R0082684291

07/2014

Dear mouse friends,
Welcome to the world of

Geronimo Stilton

THE RODENT'S GAZETTE
EDITORIAL STAFF

Geronimo Stilton
A learned and brainy
mouse; editor of
The Rodent's Gazette

Thea Stilton
Geronimo's sister and
special correspondent at
The Rodent's Gazette

Trap Stilton
An awful joker;
Geronimo's cousin and
owner of the store
Cheap Junk for Less

Benjamin Stilton
A sweet and loving
nine-year-old mouse;
Geronimo's favorite
nephew

Geronimo Stilton

THE SEARCH FOR SUNKEN TREASURE

Scholastic Inc.

New York   Toronto   London   Auckland   Sydney

Mexico City   New Delhi   Hong Kong   Buenos Aires

No part of this publication may be reproduced, stored in a retrieval system, or transmitted in any form or by any means, electronic, mechanical, photocopying, recording, or otherwise, without written permission from the copyright holder. For information regarding permission, please contact: Atlantyca S.p.A., Via Leopardi 8, 20123 Milan, Italy; e-mail foreignrights@atlantyca.it, www.atlantyca.com.

ISBN 978-0-439-84116-0

Based on an original idea by Elisabetta Dami.

www.geronimostilton.com

Published by Scholastic Inc., 557 Broadway, New York, NY 10012. SCHOLASTIC and associated logos are trademarks and/or registered trademarks of Scholastic Inc.

Text by Geronimo Stilton
Original title *Il mistero del tesoro scomparso*
Cover by Larry Keys
Illustrations by Larry Keys and Mirellik
Graphics by Merenguita Gingermouse

Special thanks to Kathryn Cristaldi
Interior design by Kay Petronio

30 29 28 27 26   14 15 16/0

Printed in the U.S.A.   40
First printing, June 2006

A LAVENDER-SCENTED LETTER...

It all started with a lavender letter. Do you like the smell of lavender? I do. It's so **relaxing**. I guess that's why they spray lavender oil at **THE REꟻTFUL RODENT**. That spa is my favorite place to unwind. But that's another story. . . .

Now, where was I? Oh, yes, the letter. That morning, I went to my office and found the letter on my desk. It was addressed to me, *Geronimo Stilton*.

Oops, I almost forgot to introduce myself. I am the publisher of *The Rodent's*

Gazette. It's the most popular newspaper on Mouse Island.

Anyway, the envelope had a letter "*S*" on it. Hmm . . . Lavender and the letter "*S*." This could only mean one thing.

The letter must be from my dear aunt Sweetfur.

Geronimo Stilton
The Rodent's Gazette
17 Swiss Cheese Center
New Mouse City,
Mouse Island

DEAREST
GERONIMO . . .

This is what the letter said:

Dearest Geronimo,

I am coming to see you Wednesday morning. There is something we absolutely must talk about!

Love and squeaks,

Aunt Sweetfur

I finished reading the letter and looked at my calendar. **I JUMPED UP.** Wednesday? That was today!

Just then, the door flew open and Aunt Sweetfur skipped into my office. She was wearing a lavender dress with a frilly lace collar. She was carrying a lilac-tinted umbrella and handbag. Around her neck, she wore a silver HEART-SHAPED locket. It contained a picture of her long-lost husband, Uncle

Aunt Sweetfur, my favorite aunt.

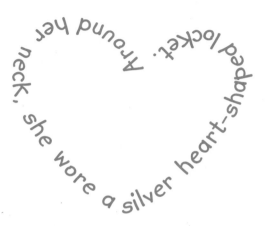

Around her neck, she wore a silver heart-shaped locket.

Grayfur. The locket held another precious treasure: a whisker that my uncle had given her as a token of his *undying love*.

Uncle Grayfur was a seamouse. Almost twenty years ago, he sailed off to the Ratlápagos Islands. He was searching for a mysterious treasure. He never returned.

Aunt Sweetfur was **heartbroken**. Can you blame her? Uncle Grayfur was her one true love. I mean, how many mice

would pull out one of their own whiskers for you? **Youch!** My snout hurt just thinking about it. Maybe that was why I hadn't found my special soul mouse yet. I made a mental note to work on my fear of whisker loss.

WHAT A DISTINGUISHED GENTLEMOUSE!

I was still thinking about my whiskers when Aunt Sweetfur wrapped me in a warm hug. The scent of lavender filled my nostrils. Oh, how I loved Aunt Sweetfur. When I was a young mouselet, she liked to read me **bedtime stories** . . . *Goldilocks and the Three Cats, Jack and the Cheese Stick, Little Rat Riding Hood.* Aunt Sweetfur taught me just how **EXCITING** reading can be.

"My dear, dear nephew! It's been such a long time since I last saw you!" she gushed. "You look so distinguished now! How wonderful!"

Actually, I had just seen Aunt Sweetfur

Once upon a time...

last Thursday. She lived in a mouse hole a few blocks away from my home. I had invited her and the rest of my family over for dinner. But Aunt Sweetfur was getting old, and her memory wasn't what it used to be.

"Ahem, well, thank you, Auntie," I said, fluffing up my fur. Did I really look distinguished? I tried to catch a glimpse of my reflection in the window.

But before I could check myself out, the door flew open.

WHAT SHARP WHISKERS!

My cousin Trap strode into the room with a smug smile. Trap runs a thrift shop, Cheap Junk for Less. When he's not at the store he loves to cook, hang out with his obnoxious friends, and play tricks on me.

"Auntie, what's shakin'? I got your letter," he squeaked, waving a lavender envelope identical to mine. **"Do you need help? I'm your mouse!"**

Aunt Sweetfur hugged him. **"Dear, dear nephew!** It's been such a long time since I last saw you! What sharp whiskers you have. And what nice, shiny fur. I bet you are very popular with the females. **How wonderful!**" she cooed.

"I have lots of sweethearts."

Trap chuckled, flexing his **muscles**. "You are quite right, Auntie, I have lots of sweethearts. Can't keep 'em away." He smirked. "Yep, when it comes to charm, you either have it or you don't. And I have it. Poor Geronimo here has got zero charm. Zilch. Zip. *Nada.* It's not his fault, really. . . . He was born that way."

I was furious. Steam poured from my ears. "**How dare you!**" I squeaked.

Aunt Sweetfur held up her paw. "That's enough!" she ordered. "When will you two learn to get along? **You have been**

fighting since you were both in high chairs!"

I sighed. She was right. A picture of messy baby Trap whacking me over the head with a spoon flashed through my brain.

Just then, the door flew open.

A picture of messy baby Trap whacking me over the head with a spoon flashed through my brain.

WHAT A SPORTSMOUSE!

My sister, Thea, the *Gazette*'s special correspondent, roared into my office. Now I was *really* fuming. How many times did I have to tell her not to ride her loud **motorcycle** inside?

Thea switched off the engine and waved another lavender envelope in the air. "Auntie, thanks for your note. **It's great to see you!** What did you want to talk to me about?" she squeaked.

Aunt Sweetfur **embraced** her affectionately. "*My dear, dear niece!* It's been such a long time since I last saw you! How pretty you look. And such a sportsmouse, too. **How wonderful!**" she gushed.

Thea grinned, twirling her tail. "Why, thank you, Auntie!" she beamed. "Did I mention I just won **FIRST PLACE** in the New Mouse City Cheddar Triathlon? I'm planning a trip to **Rataska** to go scale a glacier, and . . ."

AH, GRAYFUR!

I cleared my throat. My sister would go on all day if no one stopped her. So what if she went skydiving or won a marathon? I didn't care. Well, OK, maybe I was a little envious of Thea. The one time I tried to do a walkathon, I got so nervous that I fainted when they blew the start whistle.

"So, Auntie, can you explain why you asked us here?" I said now, interrupting my sister's rambling.

Aunt Sweetfur **CLOSED** the door. "**Well, the other day,**" she began, "**I was tidying up Uncle Grayfur's papers . . . ah, what a mouse!**" She sighed and smacked a kiss on the heart-shaped locket. Then she went on: "As I was saying, while tidying up his papers, I found a journal. It told about a treasure and a ship that was sunk near the Ratlápagos Islands. That's where Uncle Grayfur was sailing to on his last voyage. He was looking for *this* treasure."

Trap **pricked up** his ears. "Did someone say treasure?" he cried. "Well, you have certainly come to the right mouse, dear Aunt. **I'll handle this!**"

As he spoke, he reached for the journal. But Thea **BEAT** him to it. "Hold on, Cousin, our aunt needs all three of us to help. Am I right, Auntie?"

Aunt Sweetfur nodded. "That's right, dear," she agreed.

Then she pulled out the ancient journal. This is what it said:

From the logbook of Admiral Sea Snout:

Alas, what an unfortunate day this has turned out to be!

Today, Friday, February 13, 1713, at 1300 hours, my ship, The Golden Rind, has sunk thirteen leagues northeast of Cream Cheese Island in the Ratlápagos region, after hitting a claw-shaped rock.

I, Admiral Don Sea Snout, escaped with the thirteen members of my crew.

Alas, the ship's precious cargo—a chest containing thirteen diamonds as big as a mouse's fist—now lies at the bottom of the sea.

Signed,

Admiral Don Sea Snout III

"Grayfur left in search of *this very* treasure. He told me that if he could find it we would be rich, and he would never have to sail again. I miss him so!" Aunt Sweetfur squeaked, wiping away a tear.

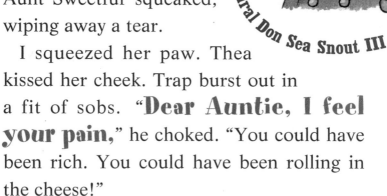

Admiral Don Sea Snout III

I squeezed her paw. Thea kissed her cheek. Trap burst out in a fit of sobs. **"Dear Auntie, I feel your pain,"** he choked. "You could have been rich. You could have been rolling in the cheese!"

Can you tell my cousin loves money?

"Oh, I don't care about the treasure," Aunt Sweetfur said. "But I do want to go to the Ratlápagos Islands. I want to visit the same places that my beloved Grayfur saw on his last journey. Will you come with me?"

Trap jumped to his paws. "Say no more, Auntiloo. **I'M READY TO SCAMPER!**" he announced. The idea of finding a treasure had put a sparkle in his eyes.

My sister checked her calendar. "For you, **dear Auntie,** I will cancel all of my appointments!" she declared.

Everyone turned to me. I had a **TON** of work to do. Plus, I absolutely hate sailing. *But what could I do?* "When do we leave?" I mumbled.

Aunt Sweetfur twirled her umbrella. "**How wonderful!**" she sang.

Right then, the door flew open.

A CHEESE HEART

My favorite nephew, Benjamin, *raced* into the room. *"Uncle Geronimo! I brought you a drawing!"* he squeaked. He handed me a piece of paper with a picture of a big yellow heart made of cheese.

"Do you like it, Uncle? I made it for you with those new markers you gave me," he explained.

My favorite nephew, Benjamin

I beamed. Isn't he the most **amazing** little mouse? Oh, how I love my dear nephew.

At that moment, he noticed Aunt Sweetfur. He ran toward her and hugged her tight. "Auntie! I didn't know you were here!"

Aunt Sweetfur kissed Benjamin on the tip of his nose. "Darling Benjamin! You are **growing** faster than a rat in a cheese shop. **How wonderful!**" she squeaked.

Trap clapped his paws. "Ahem, yes, well, I hate to break up the lovefest here," he muttered, "but let's talk more about this treasure."

I quickly explained the story to Benjamin. Then I sent him to look up the Ratlápagos Islands on the Internet.

In the meantime, I found a book on my shelf all about lost treasures. I pointed to one of the pages. "Here it is," I said. I began to read aloud:

"Admiral Don Sea Snout's ship, *The Golden Rind*, disappeared near Cream Cheese Island in 1713, at the time of the Great **CAT** War. It was one of the **biggest** ships of the time. It had thirty-six BRONZE cannons. It was last seen en route to Whiskers Landing, carrying thirteen precious diamonds for KING CHARLES CHEDDARAMA IV. No trace of the ship or its treasure has ever been found."

What a disaster! What a catastrophe! What a mystery! Did I tell you I absolutely love mysteries?

The Golden Rind

Right then, Benjamin let out a cry. "Look at this!" he exclaimed. "This agency on the Ratlápagos Islands rents out boats with a skipper. You could book a boat with an echo sounder. It's a special device to help locate objects underwater."

Thea's eyes shone. "I've got a great idea!" she squeaked. "I'll take pictures and Geronimo can write a new book. We'll call it *The Search for Sunken Treasure*. It will be a BESTSELLER!"

Trap was green with envy. "**Bestseller, bestshmeller** . . ." he grumbled.

Aunt Sweetfur patted his fur. "You are a lovely cook, dear. Maybe you can cook for us," she suggested sweetly.

"Bestseller, bestshmeller..."

That got my cousin going. He strutted around my office, waving his tail in the air. "True, true. I am a gifted chef. A genius in the kitchen," he boasted. "I will prepare some whisker-licking good delicacies!"

"**How wonderful!**" squeaked Aunt Sweetfur.

A minute later, I felt a small tug on my sleeve. "Uncle, can I come, too?" Benjamin whispered.

Our trip would be long. It would be tiring. It was no place for a little mouse.

"Oh, thank you, Uncle! You're the best!" my nephew cried when I agreed.

Did I mention I'm a pushover when it comes to my dear, sweet Benjamin?

I HATE FLYING!

Next morning at dawn, we all met at the airport. My sister, Thea, checked out her plane. Yes, my sister has her pilot's license. She also has her own pink plane decorated with flowers.

Now she patted the side of the aircraft with a loving paw. "All aboard! We're ready to hit the sky!" she announced.

Aunt Sweetfur squealed with joy. "**How wonderful!**" she exclaimed.

My head began to pound. Did I mention I hate flying?

Thea radioed the control tower. "This is **The Pink Princess,** ready for takeoff. I am heading south toward the Ratlápagos Islands."

The engine roared to life.

My whiskers began to twitch.

"You know, Auntie, I can do all sorts of tricks with this plane," Thea squeaked. **"Want to see some?"**

"Oh, yes, of course, dear! **How wonderful!**" Aunt Sweetfur cried.

My paws began to shake. "Thea, please, you know *I have a weak stomach*," I tried to protest.

But my sister just laughed. "Hang on to your tails!" she advised, *revving the engine*.

Oh, why did my sister love to torture me? I was a good big brother. I never picked on her. I never teased her. Well, there was that time when she puffed up her fur for the junior prom. She looked just like a hamster gone berserk.

I was still thinking about Thea's bad-fur-day when the plane began to **roll**. Then it did a *loop*. Then it began to dive.

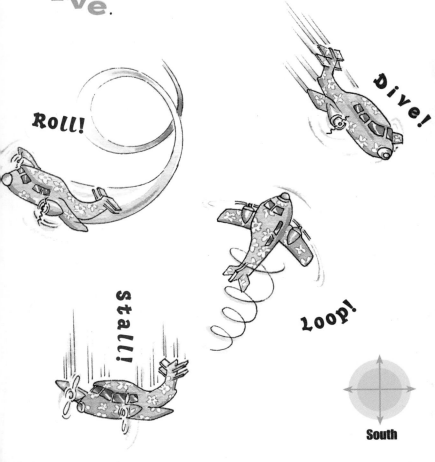

Roll!

Dive!

Loop!

Stall!

South

Then it spun through the air like a top.

"How wonderful!" Aunt Sweetfur squeaked cheerfully.

"Boring," Trap mumbled.

Amazingly, Benjamin had fallen asleep.

As for me, well, I was not a pretty SIGHT. My face had turned green, and I had used up all the AIRSICKNESS BAGS.

Ten torturous hours later, we landed. I crawled out of the plane.

"Are you OK, dear?" Aunt Sweetfur

asked me. "**You're looking a little pale.**"

I tried to answer, but I was too weak.

"He's fine, Auntiloo," Trap smirked, clapping me on the back. "Gerry Berry just loves to fly! Don't you, Cousinkins?"

Ughhh...

I wanted to **SCREAM**. I wanted to shriek. I wanted to tie Trap's tongue **up in knots** so he could never squeak again. But I had no strength left.

Just then, a suntanned rodent strode up to us. "You must be *the Stilton family!*" he said. "We've been expecting you!"

I Hate Boats!

The mouse introduced himself. His name was Scamper Skipper Paws. He was the captain of the *Queen Ratsy*, the boat we had rented. "We're ready to cast off," he said, pointing to a cheese-colored boat floating at the dock.

I moaned silently. DID I MENTION I HATE BOATS? "Ahem, maybe I could wait for you here," I suggested. I spotted a hotel near the harbor. It wasn't too fancy. It wasn't too shabby. And best of all, it wasn't floating on the water.

"But, Nephew, don't you want to see where your uncle Grayfur disappeared?" Aunt Sweetfur murmured.

Actually, I didn't. After all, my uncle was

Did I mention I hate boats?

lost at sea. He could have drowned in a hurricane, or been swallowed by a ferocious sea monster.

I was ready to hit the hotel when Trap shoved me on board. "We all know you hate boats, *Gerry Tails*," he smirked. "But it's time to face your fears. That's right. You need to get your snout out of the encyclopedia and see the real world!"

I was fuming. So what if I loved to read my *Encyclopedia Ratannica* once in a while? OK, maybe I read it every day. Can I help it if I love to read?

I shot Trap a look. He was right about one thing.

PUERTO RATO
AT LAST

The *Queen Ratsy*'s crew was made up of three mice. Scamper Skipper Paws was the captain, Milton Musclemouse was the second mate, and Tiny Tunes was the ship mouse.

Milton had a droopy mustache. He loved flexing his muscles and staring into his pocket mirror.

Tiny loved to sing. From dawn till dusk, he strummed away on a beat-up guitar and croaked out *sailor songs*. And I do mean **CROAKED**. That rodent sounded

worse than a mouse caught in a glue trap!

Needless to say, it was a long journey. Between Tiny's **screeching** and my SEASICKNESS, I almost jumped overboard. But finally, on the evening of the second day, we dropped anchor at Puerto Rato.

TRAP'S SPICY BEAN BONANZA

I was feeling awful. My stomach was doing flip-flops every time **THE BOAT ROCKED**. My snout was burned from the SCORCHING SUN. And a swarm of **HUNGRY MOSQUITOES** had decided to make camp under my fur.

Oh, why had I agreed to come on this torturous trip?

Right then, my aunt Sweetfur appeared by my side. "Are you having fun, dear?" she asked me. I nodded. What else could

I say? No, I'd rather stick needles in my eyes? I'd rather pull out all of my fur? I'd rather run naked through the streets of Cat Cove City?

Of course, the others were having a blast. Tiny was playing his guitar and screeching away.

"Rodents, keep your loved ones near.
Once pirate cats roamed around here.
They clanged their swords and
searched for treasure —
Their evil ways you could not measure.
So watch your tails, these cats are real,
They're waiting to make YOU into a meal!"

I shivered. Why did Tiny have to sing such scary songs? They were always about pirates or skeletons or ghosts. I preferred the oldie-but-cheesy tunes myself. "How

about a little cheddar boogie?" I suggested.

As usual, no one was listening to me. My cousin had jumped onto a long bench. He was kicking up his paws dancing to the music.

"**OLÉ!**" he shouted, clasping a fork between his teeth. Then he pulled my aunt onto the bench.

Ollééééé! Olllééééé!"

"**How wonderful!**" she squealed as Trap **TWIRLED** her around. When he was done he took a bow. Everyone clapped and cheered.

What skill! What talent! What a show-off!

"Are you taking notes for your book, Geronimo?" Trap **smirked**.

I rolled my eyes. If it were up to my cousin, he would be the main character in all of my books.

Two minutes later, Trap disappeared into the galley. He returned carrying a plate of beans covered with melted cheese. He offered my aunt Sweetfur a taste.

"What do you think of my latest masterpiece, Auntie? I call it Trap's Spicy Bean Bonanza," he said.

Aunt Sweetfur nibbled a tiny spoonful. "Yum!" she declared, reaching for more.

Just then, I heard a low growling sound. Was it a mouse-eating shark? Was it a slimy sea monster? Was this how it would all end? Then I realized it was my tummy. I hadn't eaten since breakfast. I was dying to

dig my paws into Trap's bean dish, but I was worried. You see, SPICY food doesn't always agree with me. Still, Aunt Sweetfur seemed fine. I grabbed a spoon. *If it's safe enough for a little-old-lady mouse, it's safe enough for me*, I told myself.

I took a tiny taste. I didn't feel a thing. And I mean **NOT ONE THING**. I couldn't even feel my tongue in my mouth. CHEESE NIBLETS! Trap's spicy beans had killed my taste buds!

And then, suddenly, I felt as if my whole mouth was about to EXPLODE. My glasses fogged up. Steam poured out of my ears. I tried to squeak, but no sound came out.

I grabbed the nearest jug of water and poured it down my throat.

"This spicy sauce is simply delicious, *isn't it, Geronimo?*" Aunt Sweetfur squealed happily. One thing you should know about my aunt, she doesn't notice much. Once, I got my tail stuck in a bottle of ketchup. I had to wear the bottle around for a week before my uncle Handypaws was able to get it off. Aunt Sweetfur never said a word.

"Ahem, yes, Auntie, it's delicious," I choked out, fanning my tongue.

AAAAGGGGGGGGGGGGGHHHH!

Trap smirked. He filled my plate to the brim. "Eat up, Geronimoid," he sneered. "You need a little **SPICE** in your life. And my Spicy Bean Bonanza will do the trick. In fact, why don't you put the recipe in your book? First, you need three tons of **red-hot** chili peppers . . ."

I felt faint. Red-hot chili peppers? No wonder I couldn't feel anything. The last time I ate chili peppers I got so hot, you could roast marshmallows on my fur.

Oh, why did I agree to come on this torturous trip?

YE OLD
SEA CAT DINER

The next morning at breakfast, Thea studied a map of the ocean surrounding the Ratlápagos Islands.

"Well, this explains why no one has ever fished out the treasure," she said. "You see, the ocean is **VERY DEEP** in this area, and the current is very strong. If you didn't know where the ship went down, it would be almost impossible to find the wreck. Lucky for us, we have Admiral Sea Snout's logbook."

We all agreed we were very lucky. Especially Trap. Any mention of the word *treasure* sent him into an **excited FRENZY**. I'm telling you, it was like the cheese had finally slipped off his cracker. He started doing cartwheels up and down the deck, singing "I'm gonna be rich!" at the top of his lungs.

Around lunchtime, we pulled into a port. We needed food, fuel, and **WATER**. I was just happy to get off the boat and away from my wacko cousin.

I took Benjamin on a tour of an **OLD FORTRESS**, while Thea went to buy water. Meanwhile, Trap said he would pick up the food.

An hour later, we returned to the boat. Well, everyone except Trap, that is. I finally  discovered him sitting at the counter of *YE OLD SEA CAT DINER*. He was stuffing his snout with **cheesy clam**

chowder and chatting with some sailors.

"Yessiree, me mateys, we're off looking for treasure. And I'm just the genius mouse to find it. The name's TRAP, one 'T,' one 'P,'" he boasted.

I groaned. When would that mouse ever

learn to keep his mouth shut? I ran up to him. "Shhhhh, you blabbermouth! No one can know about the treasure!" I whispered.

He rolled his eyes. "Hey, friends, my *lamebrain* cousinkins here says the treasure is supposed to be a secret. Is he **PARANOID** or what? Well, got to skedaddle. *Ciao!*" he called as I yanked him out the door.

We left the diner and headed back to the boat. Trap chattered the whole way. Did I mention he loves to talk? I was thinking of stuffing my tie in his mouth to make him stop. But I decided against it. I love my tie too much.

When we got back, I told Thea what had happened. She threw a fit. "YOU CAN'T BE LEFT ON YOUR OWN FOR A SINGLE MOMENT!" she shrieked.

"Well, excuse me for talking with some new friends!" Trap yelled back.

Thea grabbed his tail. Trap pulled her ears. Pretty soon, the two of them were going at it like two boxers in the rat ring.

Aunt Sweetfur sighed as she separated them. "Agh! You two are like MOLD and CHEESE. You never get along," she muttered.

You two are like mold and cheese.

CARE FOR A CUP OF SUGAR?

We sailed all night. The next morning, we dropped anchor in the bay of Cream Cheese Island.

Thea did a few calculations.
"Well, according to Admiral Sea Snout's logbook, the ship sank in this area," she said.

Just then, Benjamin gave a shriek. He was peering at the horizon through a pair of binoculars. "Look! Over there! It's the **CLAW-SHAPED ROCK!**" he cried.

Immediately, Trap broke out in a mad

series of cartwheels. But this time, no one stopped him. I guess we were all getting excited now.

Thea ordered the captain to turn on the electronic echo sounder. Our search had begun.

"Don't get too excited, Thea," warned Captain Skipper Paws. "Searching the ocean is a big job. It may take longer than you think."

For two whole days, our boat **kept up the search**. I was beginning to get worried. What if it took a whole week to find the sunken

ship? Or maybe a month? Or maybe forever? This was no place for a seasick newspaper mouse. Headlines flashed before my eyes: **STILTON STUCK AT SEA, NEVER TO RETURN: NEWPAPER MOUSE GIVES UP COZY LIFE ON LAND FOR TERRIFYING TRIP ON FLOATING PIECE OF WOOD.**

On the evening of the second day, I sat next to Aunt Sweetfur. I was feeling depressed.

"Ah, this pink sunset is so romantic! Just think, Nephew, my beloved Grayfur was sailing under this very same sky twenty years ago," she said with a sigh. A tear rolled down her fur. "Then he disappeared from my life forever."

Talk about kicking a mouse when he's down. I was more DEPRESSED than a sewer rat lost in the desert.

At that very moment, I noticed a boat floating near us. Well, it wasn't just floating near us! The boat seemed to be following us! I shuddered. Something told me the rodents on board weren't looking to borrow a cup of sugar.

SCARED OUT
OF MY WITS!

Finally, on the third day, it happened. **The echo sounder picked up something big under our boat.**

Thea switched on the magnetometer. "Yep, there's something metallic down there, all right," she squeaked.

We were all very excited.

"**Who is going to dive?**" asked Captain Skipper Paws.

Thea couldn't get into her wetsuit and **OXYGEN TANK** fast enough. "I can't wait to get some pictures of the wreck!" she exclaimed. "Who wants to come with me?"

Trap tried on a pair of flippers.

"Perfect! Just like me!" he declared.

Then he waved a flipper in my direction. "What about you, Geronimoid? Want to join us?" he asked **sarcastically**.

I **CRINGED**. Join them? Me? In the deep, dark, dangerous ocean? With the sharks and the poisonous jellyfish? Not on your life.

"Ahem, well, I think it would be best if I stayed here to look after Aunt Sweetfur," I murmured.

Of course, Aunt Sweetfur would not hear of it.

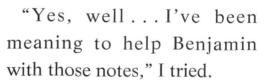

"Yes, well . . . I've been meaning to help Benjamin with those notes," I tried.

But my nephew grabbed my paw. "Don't worry about the notes, Uncle," he squeaked. "Anyway, I have a great idea.

You can talk into this walkie-talkie, and I'll record everything. You can tell us all about the sunken ship."

What could I do? With shaky paws, I put on a diving suit, a mask, a pair of flippers, and an oxygen tank. I looked ridiculous. I'm much more of a suit-and-tie kind of mouse.

"Good luck, Uncle!" Benjamin whispered.

Before I could reply, Trap pounded me on the back. Suddenly, I was tumbling snoutfirst into the water. **SPLASH!**

I was scared out of my wits. But when I opened my eyes, I saw the most **amazing** sight. I felt as though I were floating in a glass of **SPARKLING WATER**! Schools of colorful fish swam all around us. **Pink**, **blue**, and **red** coral reached up from the ocean floor. A mother sea turtle passed by, carrying her babies on her back.

Schools of colorful fish swam all around us.

"Is everything all right, Uncle Geronimo?"
I heard Benjamin's voice.

"It's breathtaking!" I replied. And it
was. Why had I been afraid of such a
fabumouse place?

Just then, I spotted something not so
fabumouse. It was an enormous fish with
whiskers. Slimy Swiss balls! It was the

same fish face I had seen in my *Encyclopedia Ratannica*.

"**CatfiSh!**" I shrieked.

I was so scared, my eyes nearly popped into my mask. Then I realized that someone was by my side. It was Trap. He shook a paw at the catfish. Then he steered me away from it.

The fish watched us go with a strange look on its face. I couldn't quite tell what it meant. Can fish laugh? If they can, this one was definitely *laughing* at us.

I didn't care. I was never *so* glad to see my cousin before. I would have hugged him if we didn't have so much diving gear on. Then I remembered he was the one who pushed me into the water in the first place. Oh, well. I guess now we were even.

We continued swimming deeper and

deeper. The water turned **COLD** and dark.
I was keeping an eye on Thea, who was surging ahead of us. All of a sudden, she began waving her paws. Then she pointed to something in front of her.

A GOLD DOUBLOON!!

And there it was.

A dark shape emerged from the depths like some MYSTERIOUS SEA MONSTER. At last, we had found the ship! I was so excited I forgot to be afraid.

Slowly, we followed Thea into the wreck. I was surprised to see it looked like it was in perfect condition. A row of cannons was mounted on each side of the ship. Under a layer of seaweed, I caught a glimpse of a faded inscription: *The Golden Rind*. A beautiful wooden figurehead hung at the ship's bow. It was a *female mouse* with wings. They say figureheads are supposed to protect a ship

A dark shape emerged from the depths.

from danger. I stared into the mouse's face. She was still smiling. I guess no one had told her she hadn't done a very good job.

Just then, I noticed Thea warning me to be careful. That's when I realized the wreck wasn't lying on the bottom of the sea. It was balanced on top of a **HUGE ROCK**. Yikes! I hoped it wasn't planning on sinking into the **abyss** with us in it. **WHAT A NIGHTMARE TO BE BURIED AT SEA.** Just think how cold it would be. And how dark it would be. Not to mention how **SOGGY** your fur would get!

I shivered as we carefully made our way

into the ship. First, we passed through a room with corroded pots and pans hanging from the ceiling. It must have been the ship's galley. Trap picked up a pan and pretended he was cooking something. I clutched my stomach. Just thinking about one of my cousin's crazy concoctions made me feel sick.

It WAS A GOLD DOUBLOON!

In another room, a row of LARGE BARRELS lay upside down along the walls. At one time, they were probably filled with gunpowder. Just then, I noticed something SPARKLING on the floor. I picked it up. It was a GOLD DOUBLOON! I quickly hid it from my cousin. I didn't want him getting too excited underwater. He might use up all of the oxygen in his tank or something. I sneaked another peek at the doubloon. It sure was shiny. I decided I would give it to my aunt Sweetfur as a memento of our trip.

We continued swimming. Finally, we reached a small cabin. A brass plaque hung over the door. It was terribly tarnished, but I managed to clean it with my paw. It read:

Admiral Don Sea Snout III

WELL, I'LL BE A MOUSE'S UNCLE!

So this was the captain's cabin. I felt so **honored** to be standing, er, well, floating there.

Just then, Thea spotted a **MYSTERIOUS-LOOKING** trunk. We managed to open it. It was **full** of gold doubloons! A smaller box contained thirteen diamonds as big as a mouse's fist! We had found the treasure!

At that very moment, I realized that something was wrong. Very wrong. Two shadowy figures peeked out from way back in the ship. No, they weren't sea monsters. They were two evil-looking rodents.

I **gulped**. Why were they spying on us?

So this was the captain's cabin.

THE DIRTY ROTTEN RODENT

The two rodents weren't moving. Probably because they were too busy watching *our* every move. It was giving me the creeps.

Thea pointed to the surface. I nodded OK. It was time to go. We'd have to come back for the treasure chest.

Of course, we had to swim up very slowly. Did you know that's an important rule in scuba diving?

As we swam, I glanced back. The two rodents were still following us!

When we finally reached the surface, I was shivering. No, I wasn't shivering from the cold. I was shivering with fear!

Benjamin and Aunt Sweetfur stared down

at us with worried expressions.

"Everything is all right!" I squeaked. No sense getting their tails in a twist just because mine was tied up in knots.

But as we pulled ourselves on board, I realized something else was wrong. Another boat was anchored right beside ours. I took

"We really, really love treasure!!!"

off my mask so I could read the name. It was called *The Dirty Rotten Rodent.*

Two seconds later, the **creepy mice** who had been following us climbed aboard our ship.

WHAT A CHEESEBRAIN!

The rodents took off their diving suits. They sneered at us. Then they burst into evil *laughter*. Cheese niblets, those two could use some serious dental work! Talk about dirty rotten rodents. I'd never seen such rotten, yellowed teeth. Hadn't they ever heard of a toothbrush?

One of them was short and ROUND with hard, mean-looking eyes. He had tiny glasses and a short tail. The other was BIG and beefy, with wiry fur. He wore a red-and-white striped T-shirt that barely covered his

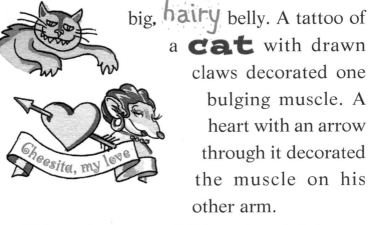

Cheesita, my love

big, hairy belly. A tattoo of a **cat** with drawn claws decorated one bulging muscle. A heart with an arrow through it decorated the muscle on his other arm.

"W-w-who are you? W-w-what d-d-do you want?" I squeaked nervously. I hoped they couldn't see my paws SHAKING like a pair of maracas.

The big mouse sneered. "The name's Greedy Whiskers. 'The Whisk' to my friends. And this here is my associate, Heartless Hairball, otherwise known as Hairy," he said. Then he laughed cruelly. "As for you, pal, I think I'll call you CHEESEBRAIN!"

I'LL RATOMIZE YOU!!

I was **FURIOUS**. I was fuming. I was hotter than my cousin's Spicy Bean Bonanza. I wanted to tell this mouse a couple of things:

1. I am not your pal.

2. Don't call me **CHEESEBRAIN**.

But I kept my snout shut. First off, I'm not much of a fighting mouse. I like peace, love, and understanding. And secondly, I was scared silly.

"So, um, why did you follow us?" I asked instead.

The Whisk's grin spread from ear to ear. Yikes! He looked like a jack-o'-lantern with those rotten teeth.

"We were at the diner. We heard your

"Cheddarface! Subspecies of sewer rat!"

friend here say he was searching for treasure. And we love treasure, don't we, Hairy?" he **squeaked**.

I glanced at Trap. He looked like he was about to explode. Uh-oh. My cousin wasn't one to hold back.

"Hey, you! Cheddarface! Subspecies of sewer rat! If I get my paws on you, I'll **ratomize** you!" he shouted, **WHISKERS WHIRLING**.

The other mouse just kept sneering. He made a farewell gesture with his paw and squeaked, "So long, **CHEESEBRAIN**!

Catch ya later, **Ratomizer**! We'll be back tomorrow to take that treasure!"

Their boat moved away and dropped anchor about ten yards from us. I guess they were settling in for the night.

Meanwhile, a **strong wind** began to rise. Dark clouds rolled in. Lightning filled the sky. I wasn't worried about Greedy Whiskers and Hairy anymore.

I was worried...

about the...

approaching storm.

A SHARK'S FIN

Within minutes, the storm hit us. Waves rocked the boat back and forth like one of those awful rides at the Wild Whiskers water park. Did I mention I get seasick?

We hid below deck, waiting for the sea to calm down. The waves grew higher and higher.

My stomach began to churn away. I felt like a furry washing machine on the super-spin cycle.

I peered inside the galley. Trap was stirring a big pot of fish fondue. "Let's see, **A LITTLE SWISS, A LITTLE CHEDDAR**, a little shrimp, a little cod, and of course, a lot of RED-HOT CHILI SAUCE . . ." he muttered softly.

I covered my nose with a handkerchief. The smell was **NAUSEATING**. Oh, why couldn't my cousin stick with something simple, like grilled cheese sandwiches or even a nice cheddar log? For a minute, I thought about making a suggestion, but changed my mind. Trap thinks he's a **WORLD-CLASS** chef. He would squeak my ear off if I interfered.

After a disgusting dinner, we climbed into bed. "Tomorrow, we dive at dawn. We must be the first to recover the treasure," Thea said.

My aunt Sweetfur wrung her paws. "**OH, MY DEARS, PLEASE BE CAREFUL,**" she pled.

"Don't worry, Auntie. We'll be fine," I reassured her. But I was worried. No, I was more than worried. **I WAS DOWNRIGHT TERRIFIED!**

The night dragged on and on. I didn't sleep a WINK. I kept thinking about the dangerous dive the next day.

Plus, the boat was pitching up and down on the waves like some crazed rat on a trampoline. My stomach was a **mess**. Still, I couldn't tell if it was due to the churning ocean WAVES, or Trap's awful cooking. This wouldn't be the first time I got food poisoning from one of my cousin's revolting concoctions.

At five o'clock in the morning, the waves

stopped crashing. How strange. It was like a magician had waved a magic wand. Now the whole sea was calm.

We put on our diving suits. I closed my eyes and took the plunge.

Before I hit the water, I heard Benjamin's voice.

"Look out, they're right behind you!" he yelled.

I glanced around. Rancid rat hairs! The two mice from the other boat were after us.

"Hey, CHEESEBRAIN!" they shrieked,

waving their paws in the air.

I didn't know what to do. Keep going? Turn back? Curl up into a ball and sob like a newborn?

I was still deciding, when I heard another shout. "*Shark! Shark!*" someone squeaked.

Just then, I saw it. A **SHARK'S** fin was weaving its way across the waves. It was headed straight for Greedy Whiskers and Hairy.

It chased them to a little inlet. They flung themselves onshore. I chuckled. It looked like those two would be spending the night on land.

I was still giggling when I saw the shark turn around. I watched in horror as it headed in my direction. Holy cheese! I swam back to our boat in record time. It was AMAZING.

I hoped my sister was watching.

All of a sudden, a loud **splash** interrupted my thoughts. I looked down. The shark swam up to our boat. What happened next? I couldn't tell you. I had fainted.

When I came to, Trap was standing over me. "Don't be such a scaredy mouse, Germeister," he said, waving the shark fin in the air. "It was just me."

I rolled my eyes. I should have known. Oh, why did I come on this horrible trip?

After a few minutes, my sister and I dove into the water again. We swam down to the wreck, found the captain's cabin, and opened the chest. Thank goodness, the treasure was still there!

Is That So, Cheesebrain?

We attached the chest to a long *chain*. Then the crew of the *Queen Ratsy* began to pull it up to the surface. Higher . . . higher . . . The chest dangled over the water. We swam after it. At last, we reached the boat and climbed on board. **PULL! PULL!!** we cried.

That's when I noticed the other boat approaching ours. **Rats!** I guess Greedy Whiskers and Hairy had figured out Trap's trick. Now they were hot on our tails.

"Too late! The treasure is already ours!" shouted my cousin from the deck.

But the Whisk just sneered. "Is that so, **CHEESEBRAIN**?"

Then, before you could say "mozzarella balls," he tossed a hook that latched onto the chest. He began to pull the treasure toward his boat.

We pulled toward our side, and they pulled toward theirs.

"Be careful!" warned Aunt Sweetfur. "If you pull too much, you'll end up with no treasure!"

Too bad Aunt Sweetfur was right.

A split second later, we heard a sharp noise. The treasure chest's lid flew open, and a shower of gold doubloons and thirteen giant diamonds rained down into the water.

The Whisk **JUMPED** in after the booty. But he got tangled up in a big clump of seaweed.

"**RATS!**" Greedy Whiskers squeaked. Hairy helped him back onto the boat, and then began picking seaweed off him. Hairy spread the seaweed out on the deck. Then he began to roll around in it.

"Just what do you think you're doing, you fool?" the Whisk shrieked.

A shower of gold doubloons and thirteen giant diamonds rained down into the water.

The other mouse just kept on rolling. "Wake up and smell the **CHEESE**, Boss. Seaweed is a natural and healthy way to soften the fur."

After a while, the two hoisted anchor and sailed away. They were still arguing with each other.

THE MYSTERIOUS AMPHORA

We all got together to squeak about what to do next.

"Let's face it, those diamonds are history," Thea began. "But we still need to explore the wreck. We need more material for our book. I say we dive again tomorrow."

We all agreed. Well, all except for Trap, who was too busy sobbing over the lost treasure. It took a pound of Chocolate Cheesy Chews, three bags of cheddar popcorn, and one large mozzarella milk shake to calm him down.

The next morning, **we dove**. Once again, we made our way through the sunken ship. That's when I spotted a strange object in the galley. It was a huge, cheese-colored, pointed **jar** with two handles on the side. It had a cork stopper that was covered with yellow **wax**.

Just then, I remembered where I had seen the object before — in my *Encyclopedia Ratannica*. It was called an amphora. Ancient Greeks used amphoras to hold all different types of liquids.

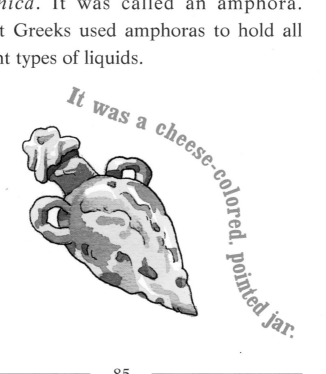

It was a cheese-colored, pointed jar.

INTERESTING, SHMINTERESTING!

Together we carried the amphora up to our boat.

"Did you find gold?" Scamper Skipper Paws squeaked.

"Did you find jewels?" Benjamin cried.

"Did you find my lace hanky? I accidentally dropped it overboard," Aunt Sweetfur added.

We laid the amphora on the deck.

"Sorry, we didn't find anything," I said. "Except for this old clay jar. It's called an amphora. It's not made of gold or precious jewels, but it is sort of interesting."

Trap rolled his eyes. "INTERESTING, SHMINTERESTING!" he groaned. "Oh,

Germeister, how did you get to be such a dim bulb? You can't write a book about a sunken ship without a treasure."

I chewed my whiskers. Was my cousin right? Would my next book turn out to be a flop?

Just then, Benjamin walked over to the amphora. "Do you know what's inside this thing, Uncle?" he asked.

"Do you know what's inside this thing, Uncle?"

HERE'S YOUR TREASURE!

I put my paw on the amphora. What *was* inside? Oil? Vinegar? SUPER-SOUR PICKLES? My tummy flip-flopped. Do you like pickles? I don't.

I tried to ignore my churning tummy as I examined the yellow-colored wax on the amphora. It had a seal imprinted on it that showed a picture of a **mouse fighting a cat**. This was the coat of arms of KING CHEDDARAMA IV.

I was still staring at the sealing wax when I felt someone shove me aside.

"**Well**, what are you waiting for, Gerry Berry?" my cousin squeaked. Before I knew what was happening, he whipped out a sharp knife and removed the stopper.

What nerve! What impatience! What was that delicious smell?

My whiskers twitched. I began to drool. The yummy smell spread throughout the boat.

Trap sniffed the jar. "It's cheese!" he announced. He sniffed again. "Wooweee! That King Ramachama really knew his cheeses!"

"You mean KING CHEDDARAMA," I corrected him.

My cousin waved a paw at me. Then he nibbled a tiny sliver of the cheese. "Cheddarama . . . cheddarlama . . . whatever his name was. This stuff is first-rat quality Parmesan, matured for more than two centuries! Here's your treasure, Geronimama!" he squeaked.

This stuff is first-rat quality Parmesan.

DON'T YOU JUST LOVE FAMILY?

I was going to mention that my name is not Geronimama, but I didn't. I was too happy. We had found a real treasure after all! It looked like our adventure was over.

That **night,** the *Queen Ratsy* headed for home. As much as I hate boats, I have to admit I was a little sad to go. The stars sparkled above our heads like diamonds in the dark sky. The ocean waves lapped gently against the sides of the boat. Maybe being a seamouse wasn't such a bad thing

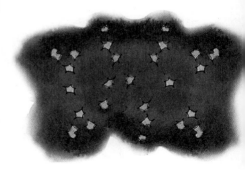

after all. Well, as long as you stayed away from those scary catfish.

Just then, Aunt Sweetfur's squeak broke into my thoughts.

"Look! Look at that falling star!"

she cried. "**How wonderful!** Make a wish!"

Without saying a word, she opened the locket she wore around her neck. The picture of Uncle Grayfur stared back at her.

My heart ached for my dear, sweet aunt. *"We love you, Auntie,"* I said. Then we all did a group hug.

I could have stayed there all day. Except Trap was standing on my paw. And my tail

Then we all did a group hug.

was twisted up in Aunt Sweetfur's umbrella. And my sister's perfume was making me gag.

Ah, don't you just love being part of a family?

family? Don't you just love being part of a family? Don't you just love being part of a family? Don't you just love being part of a family?

A TEENY-TINY ISLAND

We decided to take a different route home. "This way, we'll avoid another run-in with those two rotten rodents," Captain Skipper Paws advised.

We sailed along **a stretch of sea** where no ships ever went by. There

A shark . . . A real shark!

was nothing much to see except **water, water, and more water**. Oh, and once in a while we saw a shark. A real shark, that is. Holy cheese, sharks were scary!

SUDDENLY, far away in the distance, we caught a glimpse of a very, very small island. It was no bigger than a rock.

"How strange," Thea muttered. "It's not on the map."

Benjamin clapped his paws. "If it's not on the map, that means we're the first ones to discover it. Just like *Christopher Columouse!*" he squeaked.

Thea grabbed the binoculars. She scanned the island.

"I see three palm trees, a teeny-tiny beach, a waterfall, and one rock. I can also see a hammock hanging from two of the trees and

a tiny hut made of leaves."

A hammock? A hut made of leaves? My heart began thumping wildly under my fur.

"Cheese niblets! This means someone lives there! **A CastaWay!**" I shrieked excitedly.

My sister scanned the island once more. Then she gave a start. "A MOUSE! I can see a mouse! He's waving a yellow handkerchief!" she cried.

With a squeak, Aunt Sweetfur snatched the binoculars from Thea's paws. "It's him!" she shouted.

Two seconds later, she had **PLUNGED** into the water — fully dressed! Yep, she didn't even stop to take off her hat. Instead she began mouse-paddling toward the island at record speed.

We watched her in astonishment. Who would have thought our meek, mild auntie would turn out to be such an impressive swimmer? Still, what if she got chased by a shark? Or caught in a strong current?

"I'm right behind you, *Auntiloo*!" Trap called, jumping in after her.

"Me, too!" Thea squeaked, following Trap's lead.

I stared at the water. I really wasn't in the mood to get wet. It was so nice and warm on deck. And besides, I was having such a good fur day.

Right then, I felt a tug on my paw. "**HERE,**

UNCLE," my little nephew said, holding up a sharp spear. "USE THIS TO SCARE AWAY THE SHARKS."

I took the spear. My teeth were chattering. But I jumped overboard anyway. What else could I do? I couldn't have my nephew thinking I was a scaredy mouse.

I began swimming FOR MY LIFE.

Meanwhile, Aunt Sweetfur soon reached the beach. She raced across the sand toward the castaway, paws outstretched.

"Grayfur! My love!" she squeaked.

The mouse's eyes nearly popped out of his head. "Sweetfur! Darling Sweetfur!" he cried.

She raced across the sand toward the castaway.

THE REAL TREASURE

The two mice hugged each other tightly. I felt like I was watching the end of a romantic movie.

"Oh, my sweetie-sweetums, you haven't changed a bit!" Grayfur declared. "You are even more *beautiful* than I remembered!"

"And you are even more handsome, my grayfur-gravy-baby," she crooned.

"Oh, my pookie-pie furry-face!"

"Oh, my angel-doll, honey-whiskers!"

The two went on and on.

I wondered if one day I would meet someone and fall in love like that, too. Someone who would have eyes only for me. **Someone who I could tell my most private secrets to.**

As though she had read my thoughts, Aunt Sweetfur turned to us then. "My dearest family," she said. "As you can see, this is the real treasure —

True Love!"

Ah, love. Yes, maybe falling in love really was the greatest treasure of all. Still, I wasn't sure if I'd want someone calling me pookie-pie furry-face.

UNCLE GRAYFUR'S STORY

We brought Uncle Grayfur back to the boat. Once he was settled, Uncle Grayfur told us his story.

"Twenty years ago, I found a SMALL WOODEN BOX washed up on the beach. It held the logbook of Admiral Don Sea Snout III," Uncle Grayfur began. "I decided to go in search of what was left of *The Golden Rind*. But unfortunately, my ship sank during a terrible storm. My crew left the ship on a lifeboat. But I hung on till the last minute. I was the captain, after all. A captain cannot abandon his ship.

"When the boat sank, I managed to cling to a piece of the WRECKAGE. I was tossed around on the ocean waves like an acrobat at the Big Cheese Circus. Finally, I washed up on this beach. It's a tiny island, but I was able to survive *for all these years* on coconuts and fish."

Aunt Sweetfur KiSSED Uncle Grayfur on the snout. "OH, MY PooR SNUFFLe-MoUSe. YoU MUST HaVe MiSSeD a nice piece oF CHeese," she said, sighing.

Uncle Grayfur kissed her back. "I missed you more than cheese, *my Sugar-paws*," he squeaked.

NOT IN THE OFFICE!

We sailed home. Home, sweet home. Oh, how I missed my precious New Mouse City.

When we arrived, everyone wanted to interview us. It turned out the Parmesan we had discovered WAS THE OLDEST CHEESE SPECIMEN ever found in the history of Mouse Island! Scientists, archaeologists, and cheese experts everywhere wanted to know the details of our amazing discovery. It was a priceless specimen, more precious than gold! A sliver was put on display at the New Mouse City Mouseum of All Things Cheesy.

A plaque under the display read:

GENEROUSLY DONATED BY THE STILTON FAMILY

Our book, *The Search for Sunken Treasure,* sold like cheddar pops on a hot summer day. **A FIRST-RAT BESTSELLER!**

Of course, the book was written by yours truly, and my sister added the photographs. But I decided that we should all have our names on the cover. Aunt Sweetfur, Benjamin, and yes, even my obnoxious cousin.

It was more valuable than gold!

When Trap heard his name was on the cover of the book, he was so thrilled he started doing backflips all over my office.

Did I mention

107

my cousin is a little excitable?

"Not in the office!" I protested. But as usual, my cousin wasn't listening. He kicked over the lamp on my desk. He knocked over a stack of magazines. Then he clobbered me right in the snout.

"Not in the office. . . ." I muttered. Then I fainted.

When I came to, Trap was standing over me. He was holding an empty bucket in his paw.

That's when I noticed I was soaking wet. And I was lying in a puddle of freezing-cold water.

"No need to thank me, Cuz," Trap smirked. "A snout full of cold water always gets you up and squeaking!"

THE RATITZER PRIZE

Six months later, I was back in my office, peacefully working away. Well, actually I wasn't really working. I was reading the latest book in the RATTY POTTER series. It was so EXCITING I couldn't put it down.

Just then, there were three knocks on my door.

Before I could squeak, "Enter!" Thea, Trap, and Benjamin strolled in. They were grinning from ear to ear.

"Guess what, Geronimoid?" Trap squeaked. "We won the Ratitzer Prize! For the best scoop of the year!"

It took a few seconds for Trap's announcement to sink in. When it did, I fainted. I came to with another bucket of cold water in my snout — compliments of you-know-who. But this time, I was too happy to care. The Ratitzer Prize! I could hardly believe it! It was the most important **prize** a journalist could receive.

We were invited to a **special awards** ceremony. It was *fabumouse*. Aunt Sweetfur made the whole audience cry when she told them about *finding Uncle Grayfur* on the deserted island. Then, to mark the occasion, we each took *a nibble of cheese* from the amphora. **Yum!**

Afterward, we all had dinner at Trap's place. Have you ever been there? He lives in an **old subway train** that he converted into a cozy mouse hole. We munched on pizza from The Slice Rat. And for dessert, Thea surprised everyone with a delicious apple pie covered with mounds of steaming-hot CHEDDAR.

After dinner, I looked around the table and sighed. Uncle Grayfur and Aunt Sweetfur were giggling like two lovesick teenage mice. Benjamin was doodling a picture with his markers. Thea was touching up her pawnail polish. And Trap was, well, I'm embarrassed to say, he was picking his snout.

I rolled my eyes. Then I chuckled. *Ah, it was good to be home. . . .*

Geronimo's Joke Contest Winners!

Special thanks to all my mouse friends who sent me jokes! All the jokes were absolutely hilari-mouse. In fact, I laughed so hard, I almost broke my funny bone! Here are some of my favorites.

If a mouse lost his tail, where would he go to get a new one?
A re-tail store!
From Flannery in Washington State

When should a mouse carry an umbrella?
When it's raining cats and dogs!
From Caleb in Maryland

What animal is a tattletale?
A pig. It always squeals on you!
From Emily in Ohio

What's a mouse's favorite state?
Swissconsin!

Why do rodents like earthquakes?
Because they like to shake, rattle, and MOLE.
From Amanda in California

What's the tallest building in the world?
The library, of course! It has the most stories.

What do you call something easy to chew?
A ch-easy chew!
From Darianne in New Hampshire

What martial art does Geronimo Stilton like to practice?
Tai Cheese!
From Ryan in Texas

What happens to a cat when it eats a lemon?
It turns into a sourpuss!
From Tiffany in Florida

How do you make a tissue dance?
You put a little boogie in it.
From Zachery in New Jersey

What do you call a group of mice in disguise?
A mouse-querade party!
From the Freed family in Michigan

How does a mouse feel after a shower?
Squeaky clean!
From Ian in Washington State

What do you call a mouse that's the size of an elephant?
Enor-mouse!
From Parker

Who was the first cat to come to America?
Christo-fur Colum-puss!
From Nora in Virginia

What's black and white and red all over?
The Rodent's Gazette! It's READ all over.

ABOUT THE AUTHOR

Born in New Mouse City, Mouse Island, Geronimo Stilton is Rattus Emeritus of Mousomorphic Literature and of Neo-Ratonic Comparative Philosophy. For the past twenty years, he has been running *The Rodent's Gazette,* New Mouse City's most widely read daily newspaper.

Stilton was awarded the Ratitzer Prize for his scoop on *The Curse of the Cheese Pyramid* and *The Search for Sunken Treasure.* He has also received the Andersen 2000 Prize for Personality of the Year. One of his best-sellers won the 2002 eBook Award for world's best ratlings' electronic book. His works have been published all over the globe.

In his spare time, Mr. Stilton collects antique cheese rinds and plays golf. But what he most enjoys is telling stories to his nephew Benjamin.

THE RODENT'S GAZETTE

1. Main entrance
2. Printing presses (where the books and newspaper are printed)
3. Accounts department
4. Editorial room (where the editors, illustrators, and designers work)
5. Geronimo Stilton's office
6. Storage space for Geronimo's books

Don't miss any of my other fabumouse adventures!

#1 Lost Treasure of the Emerald Eye

#2 The Curse of the Cheese Pyramid

#3 Cat and Mouse in a Haunted House

#4 I'm Too Fon of My Fur!

#5 Four Mice Deep in the Jungle

#6 Paws Off, Cheddarface!

#7 Red Pizzas for a Blue Count

#8 Attack o the Bandit Ca

#9 A Fabumouse Vacation for Ger

#10 All Because of a Cup of Coffee

#11 It's Halloween, You 'Fraidy Mouse!

#12 Merry Christ Geronimo!

The Phantom
the Subway

#14 The Temple of
the Ruby of Fire

#15 The Mona
Mousa Code

#16 A Cheese-
Colored Camper

7 Watch Your
iskers, Stilton

#18 Shipwreck on
the Pirate Islands

#19 My Name Is
Stilton, Geronimo
Stilton

#20 Surf's Up,
Geronimo!

21 The Wild,
Wild West

#22 The Secret of
Cacklefur Castle

A Christmas Tale

#23 Valentine's
Day Disaster

4 Field Trip to
iagara Falls

and coming soon

#26 The Mummy
with No Name

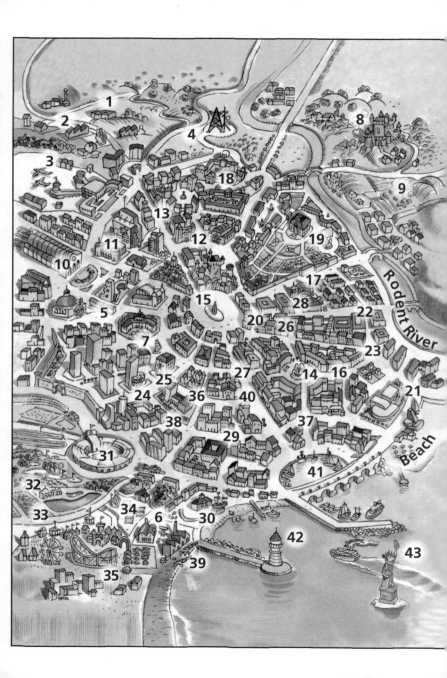

Map of New Mouse City

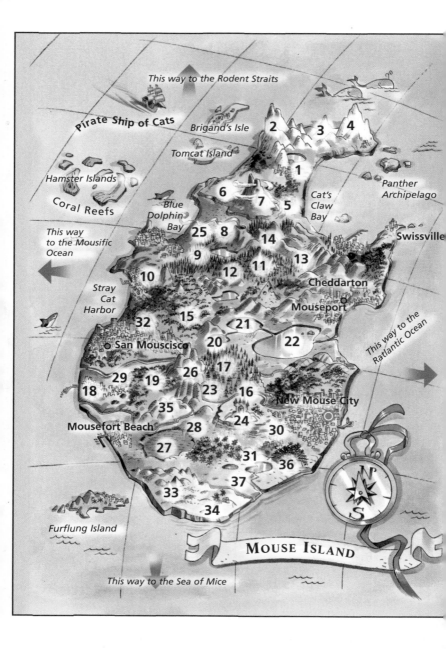

Map of Mouse Island

1. Big Ice Lake
2. Frozen Fur Peak
3. Slipperyslopes Glacier
4. Coldcreeps Peak
5. Ratzikistan
6. Transratania
7. Mount Vamp
8. Roastedrat Volcano
9. Brimstone Lake
10. Poopedcat Pass
11. Stinko Peak
12. Dark Forest
13. Vain Vampires Valley
14. Goose Bumps Gorge
15. The Shadow Line Pass
16. Penny Pincher Lodge
17. Nature Reserve Park
18. Las Ratayas Marinas
19. Fossil Forest
20. Lake Lake
21. Lake Lakelake
22. Lake Lakelakelake
23. Cheddar Crag
24. Cannycat Castle
25. Valley of the Giant Sequoia
26. Cheddar Springs
27. Sulfurous Swamp
28. Old Reliable Geyser
29. Vole Vale
30. Ravingrat Ravine
31. Gnat Marshes
32. Munster Highlands
33. Mousehara Desert
34. Oasis of the Sweaty Camel
35. Cabbagehead Hill
36. Rattytrap Jungle
37. Rio Mosquito

Dear mouse friends,
Thanks for reading, and farewell
till the next book.
It'll be another whisker-licking-good
adventure, and that's a promise!

Geronimo Stilton